The QUEEN'S Salad

Written by Abigail Flint

Illustrated by Mike Byrne

Mina was a junior chef at the palace.
She was still in training, and she couldn't
wait to make her first dish!

"I have to go out," said the head chef.
"You're in charge, Mina."

"Yes, Chef," said Mina. "I'll do my best."
She stood up straight and tall.

In strode the royal messenger.

"We need a salad for lunch," he announced. "Not just any salad – a salad fit for a queen!"

3

"A salad fit for a queen ..." repeated Mina. "I'll need the finest ingredients we have." Then she sighed. "I wish I wasn't doing this on my own."

The palace garden was full of bright light and streams of water, so it grew the best vegetables in the kingdom.

Mina climbed the trunk of the tallest tree, to reach the sweetest fruits.

She swung from the furthest branches, to pick the freshest crops.

She dug down deep under the earth, to find the most delicious roots.

Mina went from plant to plant, crop to crop and tree to tree, picking fruits and flowers and vegetables.

But as she walked back to the kitchen, one thought was going around and around inside her head:

Am I good enough to make something fit for a queen?

Mina carried a handful of vegetables to the table.

SWOOSH!

She sliced a cucumber.

SQUISH!

She chopped a tomato.

SMASH!

She crushed some seeds.

"Hmm ..." she said, looking at the dish. "That's not enough to make a salad."

But, when she reached for more ingredients, the basket was empty!

"Hey!" said Mina. "Where have all the vegetables gone?"

The clock chimed. It was nearly lunchtime!

Mina began to tremble.

"Oh no!" she cried. "This salad isn't fit for the queen!"

Then she felt a tap on her shoulder.
She gasped. There was an elf in her kitchen!

"Don't worry, Mina," said Little Elf.
"Come and see!"

The elves danced in excitement. "We did it!" they cried, bouncing from foot to foot. "We made something to fit the queen!"

Mina looked at the elves, and then at the costume. She couldn't help giggling. "Oh, Elves!" she said. "'Fit for a queen' doesn't mean a costume that fits a queen – it means 'good enough for the queen!'"

"It certainly will be good enough, once I add this last button!" said Little Elf, who wasn't really listening. He put one more tomato on the lettuce jacket.

The outfit
shook
and
shuddered ...

WHUMP!

The costume fell down
in a heap of salad.

Little Elf burst into tears.

"Don't cry, Little Elf!" said Mina.
"You made such a beautiful outfit. In fact,
all your wonderful colours have given me an idea."

She gave Little Elf a hug. "Let's pick all this up, and wash it. Then we can make a new salad together. If you help me, we'll have it done in no time."

They all worked together to select the very best seeds and stems, petals and vegetables. They chose a rainbow of colours: yellow, orange, red, purple, green, black and white.

11

Mina arranged all the different ingredients:

the flowers,

the stems,

the herbs,

the leaves,

the roots

and the seeds.

She sprinkled water over the salad to make it sparkle and shine.

"There," she said. "Now my first dish really IS fit for a queen!"

And it really was!

"Well done, Mina!" said the royal messenger. "The queen loved your salad. She's ready for dessert."

Little Elf looked nervous.

14

Mina crouched down.

"Don't worry," she said, feeling like a proper chef now.
"We'll make a fruit platter. It'll be as pretty as a picture!"

Published by Pearson Education Limited, 80 Strand, London, WC2R 0RL.

www.pearsonschools.co.uk

Text © Pearson Education Limited 2020

Written by Abigail Flint

Project managed and edited by Just Content Limited

Original illustrations © Pearson Education Limited 2020

Illustrated by Mike Byrne

Designed and typeset by Collaborate Agency Limited

First published 2020

23 22 21 20

10 9 8 7 6 5 4 3 2 1

British Library Cataloguing in Publication Data

A catalogue record for this book is available from the British Library

ISBN 978 0 435 20134 0

Printed in Slovakia by Neografia

Note from the publisher

Pearson has robust editorial processes, including answer and fact checks, to ensure the accuracy of the content in this publication, and every effort is made to ensure this publication is free of errors. We are, however, only human, and occasionally errors do occur. Pearson is not liable for any misunderstandings that arise as a result of errors in this publication, but it is our priority to ensure that the content is accurate. If you spot an error, please do contact us at resourcescorrections@pearson.com so we can make sure it is corrected.